Follow the planetary patriot @ lulu.com/spotlight/planetpatriot

First Edition: December 2012. The characters and events portrayed in this book are fictitious. Any similarity to real persons, living or dead is coincidental by the author.

The Planetary Patriot and the Day He Went to Palestine: a novel / by Edward Marcus.

ISBN 978-0-9567398-4-1

Time Travel : Science Fiction

Acknowledgments

This short work is dedicated to all the victims of the worst form of racism, nationalism, and state sponsored terrorism going. Namely Zionism! As having murdered more people then will ever be counted. And having killed more people than cancer. Said Zionism is a force of total wickedness, and a tool of the cruel. It is the most violent and aggressive form of intolerance going. But because they have Wall Street, Hollywood, the White House. Rome, all Royalty and even most "civilized" western block people in their pocket. They get away with murder and then some too...

FOR RACHEL CORRIE AND VITTORIO ARRIGONI

We all miss you so much!

I0536885

"Peace is in your hands!"

"THE PLANETARY PATRIOT AND THE DAY HE WENT TO PALESTINE"

Edward Marcus

Prologue

OCCUPIED PALESTINE AKA ISRAEL... Both valid names to the people who live there. Both names and words with letters in them that the land itself could not recognize. Or even understand. As with its indigenous biblical population on its way to being exterminated. With a policy of divide and destroy. Along with a KILL CLOCK of Auschwitz proportions silently ticking downwards. And the second non-indigenous population on its way to architecting the continued. Failing mind set of white western European manifest destiny of global rule. And equal plus one status. With even Jews of colour, being the first and original tribe of Jews undeclared second class citizens. And a version of the despicable N-Word in silent play as well. The seemingly unchallenged Zionist state of Israel stands as a walking war crime and undeclared Terrorist State! With Zionism THE clandestine global Terrorist movement.

Disgracefully backed by all major western block media outlets. (And your local and national politicians too!) With the said Zionist state of Israel being a place of shame. And collective insult to all People of the great Jewish faith... Being Apartheid South Africa on a good day. And Nazi-Germany without a final solution to the vile Jewish or rather vile Palestinian, come "Arab question" on a bad day!

As having a government that is quoted as being--"quite happy with the way things have turned out in Iraq" (How evil is that!). Having killed more people directly than Hitler. Having the major play and stake in American foreign policy. And consequently being the only country allowed to murder Americans and many other nations citizens. And even its very own without charge or mention. Along with aid workers, UN Observers, Journalists etc, etc. To getting away with oceanic hijacking of flotillas. And the shooting murders of unarmed aid workers in the head. In said international waters. This, the third most evil nation in the world (Just behind you know who! And they're not so great cousin across the pond!) always seems to be protected by many other so-called "civilized" nations because they share the same colour pigment of skin. And embrace the same immoral ideology of false democracy... Whilst as Israel always continues to be above and beyond all laws of men and God. Even when it comes to the sexual protection of its own sisters and daughters from Political attack! While taking its orders from those we do not ever see? The world itself never seems willing to stand up and say enough is...ENOUGH! That is except for just one very violent and very morally centered individual, that himself went by the name of...

ENTER THE FASTEST MAN ON EARTH...

Chapter One

A NO STATE SOLUTION FOR ONE AND ALL!

"Collective punishment works both ways!"

Seven plus hours after midnight...

T-Minus nineteen minutes precisely to launch...?

CRACK!!!!!!!!!! SLAM!!!!!!!! AND SWUNG WIDE OPEN!!! That was the sound the green painted, steel bomb proofed door made as Jackson Carter. As "The Planetary Patriot" himself entered the transgression of a hate crime. That was about to be finished with a smackdown, come beating from hell of two innocent young Arabian boys. Whose only crime was of that of walking to school. Whose only crime was being Arabic. Which sadly was enough in the stolen land and in many other "civilized" places today!

As just eight and ten years old in age. Both boys faces, that had just been filled to the top with fear and distress. Were changed to that of shock and relief! But there would be no tears! No pain! No nightmares today! As thus instantly having taken care of the problem by (Accidentally?) knocking down and out the perpetrator with the heavy door. Who was himself a misguided bully come coward, come false Jew. As way too many Israelis sadly are! The scene was now set for more actions of justice to take place...

"Stay in school!" He yelled! Yelled Jackson in Arabic, turning his head to both boys with a friendly smile. As he now ran onwards with sub superhero speed through the back morning streets...

Thus with the theme of the Kanye West track "Power" the musical setting. That itself was playing from a radio station nearby! The music! The theme and lyrics matched the scene of this violent day in the stolen land perfectly.

"ARABS TO THE GAS CHAMBER, ARABS TO THE GAS CHAMBER! DIE SAND NIGGERS! DIE!" Read much of the graffiti in the extremely run down Arabic neighbourhood. Along with a freshly sprayed. "WATCH OUT FATIMA WE WILL RAPE ALL ARAB WOMEN! AND YOUR CHILDREN TOO!"

Ignoring these misguided words of hate. That were delivered mostly in the night by the cowardly and the cruel. Jackson took no notice, having, knowing he must reach his destination without fail. As now turning a corner instantly. He now ran pass more words of things that were so vile. It would make anyone question why Hollywood movie stars with their black and brought babies. Still like to declare their love of this walking war crime of a nation.

Thus pushing onwards, delivering instant acrobatics. Jumping up and over walls. Low level buildings and objects in between, both short and tall in height. Jackson now cleared distances that no "normal" human being on Earth could do? Heading straight into a sea of incoming traffic...

A PEOPLE WITH NO FRIENDS--EXCEPT FOR ONE...
"We'll sell you guns, we'll sell you tanks, jet fighters and even twenty five mega tonne nuclear bombs. But we won't sell you real peace, maybe only a false peace, as your money's not good enough for that!"

That's who the Israelis as a collective people are. A people who have to buy their so-called friends. While one in four, that's one in four Israelis live below the poverty

line. With their streets awashed with drugs
and despair. And their young people
saturated through to their skin. And into
their very blood in pure hyper concentrated
violence.

But far too STUPID to realize it. Not
getting that AmeriKKKa and the rest of the
so-called "civilized" west, loves their
money and not them! As put in charge of the
plantation house to bring about the end of
the world with "a lake of blood" and the
third temple in the middle east. Thus
letting the End-timers ascend to heaven.
Leaving the rest of us sinners, left
behind... and left below. Israel is given
the privilege of punishing the Palestinians
aka the field slaves. For just being
Palestinians. For just being Arabian... As
with Israelis being a people themselves
still in a state of recovery. Of their very
own self caused Holocaust. Still refusing to
believe they did not resist, that they did
not fight back enough or not at all. That
they did not pick up a stone and rock an AK!
That they just put on a yellow star and let
themselves be taken away into the night like
cattle. Or rather just like lambs to the
slaughter. Now act even crueler against
Arabian people because they refuse to do the
same!!!

Thus with A NO STATE SOLUTION FOR ONE AND
ALL! Being the only way to save the day for
everyone involved. With true forgiveness.
Reconciliation and the truth, the only path

for PEACE for everyone! But with all said and done this cruel country, this cancer, this living delinquency. This sick joke upon Judaism was dying from emotional and physical pollution. From lack of water. From continuous violence. And most importantly from the non-event of much needed optimism. With the words "abandon all hope" seemingly the only phrase to sum up everything and that. But one man didn't believe that. One man. Israel's only friend (As a true friend stands against you when you're in the wrong!) was en-route to save lives on all sides and in between. As this hot morning day in the blood-soaked holy land or stolen land. Was about to get another new coat of destruction. With a weekly paint job of spilt blood! As just one angry young man sat inside a café waiting to meet his death... Making you just wonder what happens when a hundred, when a thousand. When a MILLION angry young men like himself decide to do the same???

Two minutes before...

"Make your body a bomb!" Throw away your life and take quite willingly to play along with their lying evil Government, Civilians with you! Use your body. Use your bones to cause your enemies harm. While making things worse for your suffering people! Play right into your oppressors hands. If you're in Iraq or Afghanistan. And it is against occupying family raping and child murdering coalition forces and traitors. And they are

coming to take you away to Abu Ghraib and
places much worse. The question to ask
civilized wicked people of the west is what
would you do?

But if you aren't in those particular living
nightmare of places, it very much is the
completely WRONG thing to do. These comments
of truthful confusion and pure monstrous
résistance had been running through the
young man's head earlier. That was after
watching the sunrise for what he knew would
be was the last time. Just like the tricked
hijackers themselves. This young man, who
had lost both his brothers (One of them that
was just three years old!). And watched his
mother getting almost mulled to death by a
Israeli attack dog. In a "security raid"
just two days before. Was good to go. Good
to say goodbye with an explosive "forget
you" to this cruel and uncaring world. Well
almost... As ordering the cheapest things on
the menu. Wearing a star of David to hide
his ethnicity. Knowing he could easily pass
for middle eastern and Jewish. Even though
the majority of Israelis in the stolen land
did not think much of them too. And on
borrowed time that was soon to be returned
to its owner. The young man was on his last
minutes. As people, as men and women went
about enjoying their late breakfast and
early lunches. All quite happy to stuff
their collective shameless faces. Minus two
Israeli activist leaders. Who were meeting
to discuss their next moves against their

own Government, and their "end-timer" backers.

"Don't eat so fast, Kid. You act like it's your last meal, or something!?" Exclaimed a sexy twenties something waitress walking past with a smile. "Somebody's hungry!" She said passing another customer...

Hence with the atmosphere inside filled up with the smell of cooked food and hot coffee. To conversation and noise from the kitchen. Along with a stereo playing music on a low background level. Time was just about to be up! Or was it? As turning his head to the left! Then to the right! As being a person use to going to bed hungry while hearing his mother crying herself to sleep. Watching these actions of gluttonous consumption, that in themselves just made the young man more angry. More hateful! More filled up with the emotional poison of spite itself. And more ready to carry out his "operation." His "suicide mission!" As not wanting to go to heaven in supposed and very stupid glorious martyrdom. To a place in the sky with virgins and palaces? The young man knew instinctively that there was only the emptiness of non-existence that awaited him. The END to it all. An end to the pain and daily humiliation, that was his life and his peoples life as well.

Thus unlike the cowardice of "civilized" military relying people. Having the guts and

the spine to LOOK his enemies dead in the
eyes. With those said pieces of his anatomy,
along with everything else. Including his
face. That would be ripped off his skull as
if it was a rubber mask. Would soon be both
spread upon the walls and ceiling all inside
the café itself!

"I wish I had told my little brothers that I
loved them before." Said the young man to
himself in his very mixed up and sad mind.
Crying with the pain of a lost generation.
With the pain of a people who have been
without hope for too along. "I wish I had
some place else to be! I don't really want
to die... But, but here goes!"

"Their mad, their evil!" That's what most
lying "civilized" false new world order
following people. Who don't want to really
understand would say. Not instead of asking
why? Not asking just how much would somebody
hate another person or persons. That they
would throw their own life away just to see
the them die! Using their body and their
bones as shrapnel to put their enemies down
to destruction... Thus now throwing in the
towel to his existence. Standing up and
laying down some money with the loose change
of a tip. Everything strangely seemed right?
To the said very angry young man! As being
at the most peaceful he'd ever felt in his
very violent racially abused life. All
seemed very beautiful! All seemed quite
wrongfully right!!! As almost ready to set
himself free! Free from the violence, from

the hatred and taking a few of his enemies and oppressors with him. Thus just like the proverbial Moth to the flame. He began in almost movie style slow motion to lift up his baggy white t-shirt. About to deliver one quick and hard pressed click of his suicide vests detonator! That in itself would deal out death and violent flesh ripping dismemberment ahead for all in sight?

A heart stop in motion...

LIVE FOR PALESTINE... DON'T DIE FOR IT... Was the silent message in Jackson's face as he now arrived on the scene. Entering via the back. Having jumped over a razor wired fence and straight up on the spot over a 5'11ft cook. Just as the cook himself turned around to light up a cigarette. Only to find it put out by a draft above his head? Thus with no time left Jackson was already inside the café. As with the young white T-shirt and baggy blue jeans wearing man now on his feet. It really did seem that there was no seemingly non-lethal way to save him from murdering himself and all of the civilians. Or rather all the people inside!

"TEMPORAL VIBRA-SPACE CHARGE!!!" Exclaimed Jackson having just turned the stereo up to the max. Causing all of the cafes patrons to stop! And look in the opposite direction of the young man.

As skilled in a very mysterious and frankly weird to the not knowing self-defense of the future. That gave its user superhuman abilities. Jackson put that said skill to instantaneous use, by pulling a hail Mary pass of action. As he now grabbed hold of the young man at a hyper sub-light speed. Throwing him around and sending him backwards in reverse. With Jackson himself. Crashing straight through the cafes window without even breaking it? While making the window seem that it was not made from glass at all. But instead had been replaced by a puddle of suspended water. That was frozen wet in time and space itself???

"Must be a ghost! Who ya gonna call!" Laughed the same waitresses in Hebrew again, as she now turned down the stereo.

Only for all of the patrons inside to not laugh or smirk. Not getting what she was talking about... "It was a line in an old eighties movie... Ghostbusters? Never mind! Forget it!" She uttered returning to work. Whilst all of the customers now returned back to their frothy coffee's and etc. All not realizing or even seeing what spectacular events had just transpired, and then some.

Outside and high above...

As now opposite the café on a flat roof top next to a fire escape. Having disarmed the young man, removing his "suicide" vest! Disarming its Mossad remote chicken switch as well! Jackson stood tall over the situation! That is 6'3 tall... While apparently a white male aged in his very late twenties to just early thirties. And having been on a running assault. He now strangely showed zero sign of sweating in the morning heat.

"This is not the way!!! There's no path to paradise by doing this."

"I don't want to go to Paradise." Uttered the young man. "I just want it over, and I'll take some of them with me."

"That's what they want at Langley and M.I.6! Their Mossad and their Endtimer masters. They keep setting you up to keep doing this!" Jackson snarled with base in his American-English accented voice.

"What would you, know! You're American, your white! You wouldn't..."

"Am I?" He remarked as his skin now weirdly changed back to his true colour. That being of a light brown skinned, black man. "O' back to usual!"

"How did you? What are you...?"

"A friend! Now..." Said Jackson only to stop
mid-sentence realizing that something else
was about to be happening real soon?

STOP THE CLOCK! TEMPORAL FLASHFORWARD...

Seeing into the future! That is the future
just less than an hour from now. Jackson
witnessed the atrocity! Witnessed the
business of usual. Witnessed the slaughter
of a group of innocent Palestinians who had
all been shot, crushed and blown apart by
Israeli "Defense" forces. Along with private
mercenaries brought in for a free practice.
As with the children amongst them all
disappearing without a trace. Taken away to
fates far, far worse than death itself... As
having less mercy than Hitler's Germany
themselves. With even their victims granted
the eventual death of mass murder in the gas
chambers, and other still classified
horrors. The Zionist state of Israel is a
AmeriKKKan come western block backed
monster. An "abomination" as one brave and
true Jewish Rabbi had the courage to say. A
pure soul swallowing predator. Who sadly
enjoys to play with its food, with its prey.
As having subjugated the Palestinian people
and others for over sixty years and
counting. Not having the guts like Adolf
Hitler to just get it over with. To just get
the job done and complete their final

solution to the Palestinian and the Muslim question as well.

"There still going through with it! I knew they would, Motherfuckers!!! KNOWING--Racist Nazi wannabe, Apartheid worshipping House slave--Motherfuckers!" Cursed Jackson with a fast spoken growl. Snapping out of just one of his countless strange and superhuman abilities... "You know..." Remarked Jackson taking a momentary pause. "At the end of the day collective punishment works both ways!"

"I wish!"

"Ask and you shall receive!" Was the silent look in Jackson's eyes as he now turned to the young man. Putting on his newly acquired suicide vest himself?

"Go home, son! Go home!"

"I--don't have one!"

"Don't worry... You will soon... You will soon..." Jackson uttered with near big brother assurance. Placing a note with a printed address on it, into the young man's shaking hands! That was to a safe house run by real Jews, by true Jews in the stolen land!

"Now get lost and go to this place... And when you get there, stay indoors! Cos otherwise son, you're going to catch cold???"

"Catch cold?" Said the young man, quite confused.

T-Minus sixteen minutes to launch...?

WHAT IS ZIONISM...? Corruption! Greed! Apathy! Pure Power! Pure poison! White Judaic racism, white Jewish Power. The Synagogue of Satan of revelations! A free pass to use the wicked term of the N-Word and worst! A free exception to even call for the expulsion of not just the ingenious Arab native people but also black Israelis too. Who themselves have strangely falling birth rates. With even so-called mixed race children of white and black people in the stolen land. Considered taboos at best and abominations at worst!

Thus THE most hardcore white racist movement on the planet. That can give good old boys in white sheets in eighteen eighties Amerikkka a run for their money and win. With the Zionist state of Israel or IsraHELL as some say. The best example to what white power really is and then some. That is Zionism! That is the Jewish state and "Jewish" movement! That in all, that in other words adds up collectively to be false Judaism!

As working for the original backers of Hitler! Nazism without world war two and if it had made it to Hollywood. (As they almost nearly did!) "Sieg heil" with a twist of family friendly mouse loving entertainment corporate backing! A fascist movement that advocates extreme nationalism and unquestioning authoritarianism! That sets about to murder and ethnically cleanse the world of the original founders of its faith. That poses as a protector of traditional national culture and religion.

That itself spends more money on death instead of life. That allows only "Jewish" people to own ninety percent plus of the land. With railroads in construction (That sounds familiar?). With more and even more illegal settlements in progression. That glorifies violence, torture, and promotes populist right-wing economic programs of Judaic living space etc, etc. As standing in violation of more UN resolutions than ANY OTHER NATION ON EARTH. Not realizing due to their House slave status to the overseers known as America. And their boss and masters the U.KKK. That if they just accepted just half of the said UN resolutions that they would have found at least a viable way to peace. The racist movement that is Zionism's mission statement of practice being NEVER AGAIN! Would be better served up by saying-- NEVER SAY NEVER?

MISSION OF JUSTICE IN PROCESS... A suffering people in a state of recovery after getting thrown into boxcars and then into camps, gas chambers and ovens. Too being made into lamps, tables. And yes, even bars of soap! A suffering people because they have lost their humanity! Lost their respect for their great religion... Ghettoizing their neighbours and themselves. Muddying the river of the great religion of Judaism. With an open sewer of injustice that is the Zionism. Having shamed Anne Frank and all of the twelve million plus victims of Hitler's death camps. As with Zionism brought in a living reality, forged into being by terrorism and the will of a lost people that suffered so greatly at the hand of the Hitler's Nazi-Germany. They themselves have lost their perspective on truth! On justice! As with their once great moral compass having melted away inside heart of the monstrous ovens of Auschwitz and Belsen...

The sky high majority of Israeli citizens are far too comfortable in the well worn-out shoes of racism, hatred and cold blooded murder. Even when it comes to that of children. As having an undeclared secret record of torture, and numerous other atrocities against the innocent or the held without charge... Forgetting that every action has a reaction. And that if you push people enough, some days they'll push back!

JUMP TEL AVIV... JUMP JERUSALEM... JUMP THE WALL... Death defying in completion and execution, with running step, after running step delivered with hardcore heaven perfection. With--"Justice, justice, you shall pursue!" The running Torah quote of these seconds. Of this single minute in pursuit against these good ol' boys with gunships. As skilled to the maximum in the extreme sport of "Free Running!" Jackson slammed downwards over flights of stone steps like a metal spring. Only then jump and bounce sliding over and leaping through tighter than tight. And narrower than narrower fences and barriers... Coming towards large number of checkpoints...

"Life in a Prison! Life in hell! Backed by Washington, London and Rome all the way." Humiliation... Embarrassment, mortification, shame, the threat and execution of violence... Fifty plus checkpoints. Pimp slapping old people like Nazis in Poland. Mothers giving birth, the sick dying, Children suffering, ethnic prejudice in practice! (i.e. Making sick leukemia victims get out of their cars and walk off their chemotherapy till they die!) Along with IDF girls putting their hands were they should not upon boys aged just twelve for camera phone recorded giggles and "fun!" Power over other Human beings in conclusion! These were just a million ways and words to describe what it feels like and what events transpire at these crossings of degrading racial segregation. That would make even a nineteen fifties deep South living, white false Christian bigot--ashamed! (Just a little bit!) As with queues of People, of men, of women, of children. Stopped and doubled stopped. Checked and double checked, just for fun by Israel Soldiers. With their only protection being from beyond brave Israeli feminists groups and unrecognized others... That themselves get the return privilege to be called "Whores and traitors" by their own countrymen.

One second onwards...

With Jackson himself having just completed a POWER MOVE of his mysterious martial art. That itself went by the most extraordinary name of Te Vu'Kra - Fu! That now had just caused him to clear all of the guarded checkpoints, within under a blink of a single eye! Going unnoticed as if he wasn't even their...? With TIME itself seemingly coming to a near frozen STOP! A path towards a collection of illegal settlements lay just ahead...

FUCKING POSERS... "We build roads from village to village, from town to town, we create new lands for the farmers' fields and forest acres and bread for ~~Germany~~, for Israel." The mission statement of Zionism. The mission statement of Hitler's Nazi-Germany too. As thinking the way they live is okay. With their children given permission to racially abuse their

neighbours children to the maximum! Along
with quotes of--"It is okay to kill people
as long as you're wearing a military
uniform! (Meaning that? O' dear!) With cries
of-- "European! Jewish! European! Jewish! Of
Holocaust! Holocaust! Auschwitz! Auschwitz!
Anne Frank! Anne Frank!" Mixed together with
a - "You just take it! What did they ever do
with it! And what has Islam ever given the
world!" Making you get the weird sense of
déjà vu nineteen thirties Germany style! As
basically the KKK with the U.S 82nd airborne
division on super speed dial for murderous
support... The so-called permanent
settlements, just like the "Christian"
pilgrims, disturbingly represents the
phrase--EXPAND OR DIE to the max..."

Thus with more cries of "Jew haters, Jew
haters. And they are savages, they are
savages! This is our land, God said so!" As
with the said illegal and constantly in
construction settlements in monstrous and
ever growing proportions. False Judaic
lebensraum was indeed in full practice...
With--"We need living space, we need
breathing room!" (More like killing space!)
On full military supported fulfillment. With
the out spoken need for land and an already
planned out great Israeli expansion into
other places. From Egypt to the Jordan, to
Syria. To the Lebanon, the Yemen and back up
to Iraq! In the not to distance future. With
many settlers, but not all!(Well just about
ten, but that counts!) Happy to see
Christianity and Islam in a battle and war

of almost Mutually Assured Destruction. Not realizing that they will be set to burn too.

T-Minus twelve minutes to launch...?

FASHIONABLY LATE IS NOT AN OPTION... Was the call of play. As with a facial expression of a would-be white rabbit that was running late to meet the Queen of Hearts! Come a man who was late for a hot date with his even hotter girlfriend! Jackson ran up the side of a wall only to then speed forwards running a straight line without even putting his arms out for balance? Delivering mad moves of dynamic amazing Spider Man styled dexterity. As now doing cat leaps and forward no hands cartwheels. And being a master to the infinite degree in the aforementioned extreme sport, or rather the extreme urban art of FREE RUNNING. Of PARKOUR! This lightening charge ahead was a walk through the proverbial park, and then some for him, as he now headed downwards. Jumping instantly into the crime of trespass. Travelling through a number of backyards, gardens and swimming pools... Just as a middle aged woman, who herself was wearing a bathing suit that was a number of sizes too small, had finished preparing a tray of drinks...

Therefore seeing an impossible sight, even in this supposed holy land. That in itself had not been seen for real in nearly two thousand years. The woman now witness

Jackson walking! Or rather running on water. Speeding over the deep side of her swimming pool as if he was running over solid, yet wet ground???

"Shalom!" He exclaimed in perfect spoken Hebrew, to the woman who was carrying the said plastic blue tray of drinks... Only for her to now DROP them, in seeing the said impossible!!! As now jumping upwards high into the morning sky, exiting the settlements. Jackson headed towards the incoming scene of the undeclared war crime...

Now landing with high falling yet safe landing of a perfect gymnastic ten. Jackson was on the wall and about to be OFF THE WALL! That is the villainous hardcore racist in statement and rightfully named Apartheid wall. That goes by the name of the security wall by the world's so-called "civilized" people!

"Here we go again!" He said to himself aloud, perched like a gargoyle. About to enter full "Insurgent" mode! About to do his dirt, his days' work in the SKI MASK way! About to take on the "might" of the Israeli military itself!

Chapter Two

COWBOYS AND INDIANS ALL OVER AGAIN!

"No such thing as an unbeatable enemy!"

One minute onwards...

THE WEST BANK AND GAZA... Suffering from
real Anti-Semitism. Suffering from
everything and anything that one group of
Human beings, with ultimate power over
another group of human beings could use. And
throw against them! From murders completed
in all forms. From sniper shots to the head
and especially the neck. To cut throats in
the dead of night. From the war crimes of
white phosphorus bombs aimed directly at
women and children! To state approved
torture, house rapes, lynching's and even

worse things to vile to mention against
children as well. Through to crimes against
even the environment of Palestine itself. In
the form depleted and non-depleted uranium
bullets alike. From raw sewage and
radioactive waste! To a food shortage and
water shortage as well... Thus sending hope
on holiday, a very seemingly permanent
holiday and state sponsored vacation! All
things were about to become strange?

As with buckets! Buckets! And more very
mysterious buckets placed outside and on the
roof tops, all throughout the west bank of
Palestine and Gaza too? (Just like some
master piece of world art!) Colours of
luminous green, yellow, blue and orange.
With reds and a few purple's thrown into
living mix of new art as well. Thus making a
very spectacular view from high up and above
in the blue cloudless morning day...

Back down on Earth...

WAR CRIMINALS ON THE JOB... Just like Iraq,
just like Afghanistan. And countless other
undeclared places. True terrorism!
Atrocities, suffering and "legitimate
genocide." Were on the cards for a group of
people who never counted as Human beings
anyway. Which is sadly the norm for way too
many people of so-called colour and those
without monetary privileges. As with the war
crime of search and detain being put into
practice. And parked armoured vehicles with

back-up Tank support on the way... All was set and in play. As on the edge of a smashed and half broken residencies (If you could call it even that.) a group of mostly women and children, where being rounded up for "questioning?" With the real facts on the ground being that they were heading for an Abu Ghraib every day. In the custody of "Civilized" western block democracy styled individuals.

"You fucking dirty rag head Arab bitch..." Said the Zionist Stormtrooper. Ripping off her head scarf, ripping off her hijab. Only to go even wickedly further. Slapping the fourteen year old girl in the face. Sending her crashing down to the sandy soiled dirt...

"You dirty whore. I'd do you myself, but I don't know what I'd catch." He voiced showing himself to be truly inhuman filth, being the IDF at its best! "Maybe we will send you onto the Americans and the British. As they like to rape Muslim bitches like you for breakfast..." He laughed as another Stormtrooper grabbed hold of her little brother who was just only eight years old.

"Yeah you can send your little brother! As they like to show little Arab boys a good time too!" Laughed the other Stormtrooper. Enjoying the pure fear and wickedness of their unchecked power. As another turned away in silent disgust!

"Yeah you little... What is it the Americans call them?"

"Box Cutters?!"

"No... The other! Hadji?" He voiced getting it himself. "Hadji Girl! Durka, durka, Jihad, Jihad!" He laughed with that giggle that all racists do. Copying an infamous line of Zionist movie media quotation.

Thus with that "I am better than you" racist loony look in his eye. He now spoke with even more Zionist vile. "When we get you back to base." He uttered taking out his specialized iPhone... "You are getting the strip search from hell. You little hot rock throwing slut!"

While now still on the ground, as the laughter and giggles of war criminals and rapists heckled outwards. The young girl felt nothing but fear and pain, knowing that--that things were about to get even worst for herself. Her brother and the other people there as well. Or were they...?

One single split second later...

"ALLAHU AKBAR!!!!!!!!!!!!!!!!!!!!!!!!!!!!!!"
Jackson Screamed in Arabic in full insurgent

mode. Declaring as many know that GOD IS
GREAT and then some. Therefore mimicking a
resistance fighter's call to action. And
self-defense of his nation and people.
Against western block fanatical mineral
wealth grabbing. And forced war nation
rapists aggression. As like the sight of the
fictional comic book hero Batman's
appearance of a giant bat creature, in the
shadows of night. Jackson's look and perfect
pronunciation did indeed also instill pure
fear, and dread into the hearts of all men.
And women of evil as it did here. As now
just one broken nose and a fractured skull
later. The facts where completely
conclusive, as the said IDF Stormtrooper.
Who had struck the fourteen year old girl.
Had just got one quick and very sharp KICK
to his face. Giving him a much needed call
for complete facial reconstruction, and a
lifetime addiction to painkillers.

While just before the Stormtrooper even fell
down. Jackson was on the ground off and
running! Unleashing just one quick spin kick
that send five more Zionist thugs face down.
With no teeth, out for the count.

"Get here you little sand nigger bastard!"
Yelled and snarled the surviving villain,
pulling out his side arm. As he now grabbed
hold of the little boy, about to use him as
a human shield.

Now showing what the true meaning to the
word bully, coward and Zionist meant. The
IDF Stormtrooper now quickly pulled out his
gun placing it next to the little boys head.
Ready to pull the trigger! When he now
looked up to see that Jackson was not in
front of him and his position?

"Shit! Where is he...?" He yelled not even
realizing that "The Planetary Patriot"
himself was standing right behind him, as if
by magic...

Screaming blue bloody murder, as his arm was
simultaneously broken in two places by just
one fast snap of Jackson's hands. Dropping
his gun! This wicked man got to know
actually what a hand grenade tasted like...

As taking one of his said grenades Jackson
SLAMMED it straight into his vile mouth.
Breaking half the Stormtroopers teeth in the
process! Only to then frog march him
forward. Throwing him straight ahead into
back of the armoured vehicle. Swinging the
door shut while turning in one single fast
motion. Grabbing hold the young boy, and
lifting up the slapped girl with his other
arm.

Escaping them both to quick safety as the
grenade in the Stormtroopers broken mouth,
detonated with a metal clunking
BOOM!!!!!!!!! Killing him instantly. While

the armoured vehicles structure kept the blast inside the said vehicle. Completing the "put a gun to a child's head--hurt a child in anyway and you're a dead man philosophy of--"The Planetary patriot!"

Thirty-three seconds onwards...

THE PLANETARY PATRIOT IS HERE! A man who stands up! A man who stands UP for others when no one will. As thus left in a vacuum. Left to go hungry and left to go cold. With no Hollywood "liberal" trash to be seen in sight! With all of the "Phonies" and all the others staying away because they're not down with that colour of brown yet. Because they don't score any points yet too! As being the American Indians before Custer. The good people of Palestine have suffered the most in the past and current present. But today was a different day! As saving the two children, Jackson now took off his ski mask so not to frighten the youngsters.

"You both okay? Here let me look at you young lady!" He very kindly said, as now showing that his strange and very much fantastically skilled Te Vu'Kra - Fu. (That also had the alternate name of the martial art of murder.) Was also about healing the human body and not just destroying it.

"All better now, sister! All better!" Said Jackson as her split bloody mouth and

bruised cheek was now all healed up
completely. With him now picking up the
young girls hijab, handing it to her, as if
he was her older brother...

"Shukran!" She said saying thank-you in
Arabic. She said smiling a true smile like
the innocent child she was. As she fixed her
hijab...

"You're welcome, little sister... You're
welcome!" Thus now with the back-up formerly
on the way, as clouds of dust and engines
grinned through the hot and getting hotter
morning day. More battle, more combat was
now about to put be into play...

"We want to fight!" They both said, showing
what the words true courage and resistance
really meant. As they both each picked up a
lone and solitary rock! As if both stones
were laid out for them to do so...

"Thanks for the offer kids, but today or any
other day's not a day for you to die... Now
go to your people and tell them to stay
BEHIND the hill over there, and take cover
okay!"

"Okay!"

"I mean it kids, stay down!"

"We will."

"And remember, Kids. Real Muslims live for
Islam, they don't die for it!" Declared
Jackson, giving them the wisest words he
could give!

"Okay! But wait!? What's your name?" Voiced
the young girl.

"My name...? Well some call me--the fastest
man on earth! But for the life of me, I
can't think why...??? TEMPORAL RAINING RUN!"
He then exclaimed only to vanish. Jumping
into a burst off super near sub-light speed
head. Straight towards danger once more...
While at the same time leaving both children
mesmerized.

T-Minus eight minutes to launch...?

Bat Shalom (Women for Peace), Breaking the
Silence, Courage to Refuse, Gush Shalom
(Peace Bloc), the Israeli Committee Against
House Demolitions (ICAHD), Machsom
(Checkpoint) Watch, Physicians for Human
Rights, Rabbis for Human Rights, Ta'ayush
(Arab-Jewish Partnership). Yesh Gvul (There
is a Limit) and Zochrot (Remembrance). List
and names of the "extreme minority" that are
Israelis only Jews, minus a few more silent
and sadly nameless heroes. But the men and

women that Jackson were about to take on were anything but that. They were the negative words to good, kind and courageous. They were nothing but Centurion styled Stormtroopers in service to wicked individuals of evil. Backed by beyond insane false Christian End-timers. And a FAKE New World Order. That itself belonged to a secret illuminati of unchecked global elitists. As with children having sniper shots to the head. Babies thrown from windows, pregnant women kicked till they miscarry. Being just a few of the silent and never brought to justice crimes against humanity that Palestinian's along with Lebanese people have had to endure... This impending war crime was now in the progression of being cancelled...

THE ABUSED BECOMES THE ABUSER... Was theme as bullets inside M16 semi-auto rifles locked and loaded ready to murder. As the first wave of IDF (Israeli Defense Forces!) Stormtroopers took aim for a 6'3 ski mask, suicide vest wearing Terrorist!

Terrorist! Such a strange label, a weird label! A label of violence, of semantics of total racist western block hypocrisy. Of-- "That man, that terrorist! Of its okay to invade sovereign nations like Vikings on lies. And then occupy them like Nazis in Poland. But if you fight back in total self-defense not wanting to get raped, not wanting to get murdered in your own home. You're guess what?--A terrorist!"

But never the less, it was a label that Jackson himself was comfortable wearing. With that said word "terrorist" being actually what he was in his shameful war criminal past. While at the same time that said word just bouncing of him like bullets of Superman. As he knew he was in good and bad company alike. From Jesus to Mandela! Onto Bin Laden, Bush, Blair and the guys and girls, "the actors" in so-called charge before and after them alike also. As to him, the word terrorist was made up of nine letters and didn't really mean much more than that! While in reality he preferred a group of just three words that went a little something like...

"TEMPORAL NOVA CYCLONE!!!" Jackson now declared in loud vocal declaration! As turning himself upside, and in fast rotational assault. He now spun around, around and around hundreds of time per revolution of the just ticking by seconds. Defying gravity itself.

Thus avoiding a rapid burst of semi-auto fire. Even though he really didn't need to. He now scooped up the villains. Making it look like a twister had dropped from the cloudless sky. Sending all of the IDF Stormtroopers airborne, cast up, thrown about and all around. Only to then be accelerated with a body breaking SLAM into each other, knocking each other out for the complete unconscious count!

Having broken jaws and bloody noses, laying down on the job... These misguided individuals were beaten by the best! By the fastest man on earth. By "The Planetary Patriot!" As now back down on his feet and still running. Jackson went straight ahead as another wave of enemies (Not seeing what he had done!) charged at him with handguns and clubs drawn. Not realizing that they were delivering him the hand to hand advantage...

"Son go cut me a switch and I'll take these naughty little Zionists to the woodshed for ass whoopin'!" That was the lesson of the moment that was in full schooling! As with the universal right to education denied by said Zionist aggression and sixty years plus occupation. The two children were now getting home schooled. With today's class being... "How to stand up for yourself against racist false Jews."

Therefore with Jackson himself getting an A plus grade. As built like a brick house with fists of black steel, fists of fury, of justice to match. That were charged with the will of the almighty one himself! As holding back so not to deliver instant death with just one strike! Jackson now did lay the provably smackdown against the incoming villains, man and woman and battle Tank alike.

Many moments of violence onwards...

TANK DIVISION DEFEATED... Supposedly battle hardened. Supposedly the best! (Yeah right!) As not believing in a fair fight just like a heavyweight champion beating up on a paralyzed from the neck down kid in a wheelchair. The Israeli military, just like its western block masters. Were pussycats, and weak minded lily-livered cowards to say the least. As now using the largest and heavy set males amongst them. Jackson now set about with superhuman strength to knock down the incoming Stormtroopers with brute body lifting force. Breaking them down and sending them all falling over. As if the incoming evil doers where ten pin bowling pins...

"Strike!!!!!!!!!!!!!" Was now the silent and quiet cheesy expression, which could not be seen through his ski mask. As with all of the IDF Stormtroopers knocked down and out! Jackson lowered the remaining villain to his dizzy feet about to walk away...

Thus if all of this had just been a children's cartoon. Seeing stars, with little birds flying around his head. Would have been the situation for the dizzy-wizzy Stormtrooper. But this wasn't! As now turning to walk away Jackson would have a funny moment anyway. As he now turned his head and pretended to blow down the villain. As if he was blowing out a single candle. Instantly falling down the Stormtrooper was also out for the count. As more danger was about to be upon Jackson himself...

THE PRIVATE SECTOR IS IN THE HOUSE... Those mercenaries that have changed in name only. That from Iraq and Pakistan and all between (And Libya off the books too.) specializes in doing mass murder. That specializes in doing mass rape! And mass lynching's of children too. At super cuts rates. On the go and say so of your president and prime minister too! That also cut babies from pregnant women's stomachs just like in the days of Indian wars. To the late vile Sharon in the stolen land as well. Were now on the scene armed to the teeth with weapons outlawed and not known to the general public. Said weapons that might even defeat the planetary patriot himself?

Nineteen seconds later...

"ALLAHU AKBAR!" Jackson had yelled as dead! Dead and yeah the last guy had just been killed, murdered where he stood by the fastest man on earth. By the only man not afraid to send all western block crusaders rightfully home in body bags. Private sector or regular armed nation rapist forces too.

As knowing whether a "hero" screams for his mother when his throat is cut. Or his sovereign of a nation rapists! Jackson had destroyed these war criminals. With their said weapons of advanced technology causing no problems for him and then some... Only for now like a next round of a video game for more trouble. More villains to come his way, in the form of Earth moving machine laying just ahead...

"Do you want to be a white racist? Do you want to be a science experiment gone crazy?" Don't be a Nazi, don't be in the KKK, or one of those M.I.5 sponsored British fascist groups. As those guys, as all those losers are yesterday's news. The best they can do is get permission and blow-up a federal building and kill innocent people. Or sell drugs to their own communities, or pimp out their white sisters. And get their white brothers sent to a super max prison. To bitching about immigration and Islam on TV.

No! If you really want to be a white racist, for the moment? Be a Zionist! You'll have to put up with some people who aren't white. But you can have the President. Have the prime minister or any other war criminals across the globe. Back you as long as the cheques are in the mail. You can be a head Rabbi and stand in London waving a flag calling for the Lebanon to be set to burn. Why you can even get your very own holocaust for sixty years plus in the Middle East. And come TV and deny the body count in Iraq!

Call any true Jew who stands for the truth and thus against you, a traitor, a communist and a sell-out. And have them be the victim of a stray bullet or a car crash! Go to the U.N and call for "something" to done about Iran! No! Call yourself Jewish but not really mean it. As no one Jewish, no one who would believe in the word of Torah would be that way. Would believe in collective punishment. In torture, in atrocity. In human destruction and the murder of children! That's what was in continuous practice here. As running as if his very own life depended on it (Even though it did not!). Jackson went straight towards one of three incoming Bulldozers.

MAN Vs MACHINE... Machine should always win? That was the most sensible thing to say. But life and the real living reality of the world was almost and will be anything but! As Jackson now leapt forwards...

"TEMPORAL CONCUSSION KICK!!!" He yelled showing a working demonstration of a power move. That instantly smashed the front of the bulldozer. Knocking out its driver and breaking it apart from the inside out...

One down two to go! As with two more dozers that themselves looked to the unknowing person that they were from the near future. Built for construction work on the moon itself. Or at the very least straight out of a murderous, bloody violent video game. The said dozers now approached revving up their diesel engines, with grinning ferocity...

"He's just one man. What can he do?"

"He's done for!" Said one of the Palestinian refugees. Who was taking cover with the two children by the hillside...

"No! He's not!" Said the young girl back. "He's not afraid... He is not afraid!" She now uttered with a whispering hush, looking towards a distant Jackson!

Earth moving machinery! House destroying, homeless making, collective punishment Zionist racist, fascist metal monsters. Built for crushing and murdering Christian and Jewish American peace activists. Built for stealing land on false birthright. This was just one of the many verbal ways to describe the Bulldozers used in the stolen land. As with two left, Jackson ran head on into danger. As the said Bulldozer let rip with a burst of full auto mini gunfire... Dancing a dance of gymnastic skill. Jackson dodged the incoming supersonic rounds of vile depleted uranium bullets! As now jumping back to the earth it now seemed that he had indeed met his match...?

"I got him... I got that Muzzie bastard!" Yelled the Bulldozer driver into his

radio... "He's flat as a pancake! He's...
What the? O` shit!!!!!!!!!!" He now screamed
as his Bulldozer was sent flying up of its
super heavy caterpillar tracks!

"Lift with your legs!" And lift with his
legs he did. Bench pressing a few tonnes of
metal, of machine... As sending the
Bulldozer onto its back like a sea swept
turtle. Jackson showed that he was a man who
was capable of some amazing feats of
strength. As back up on his feet, he now
went airborne again. Landing on top off the
last remaining dozer...

T-Minus five minutes to launch...?

"I don't see him...I don't see him?"
Screamed the driver in fear of just seeing
the impossible... "O' dear!" He yelped as
the hatch was now ripped open, as if it was
made of just gift wrapping paper...

Ejected by "the most angriest man on the
planet" by Jackson himself. And nearly
messing his pants at the terrifying sight of
a snarling ski masked resistance fighter.
The cowardly driver ran away from the scene
of the crime. As in control of the said
Bulldozer, having hijacked the vehicle for
his own personal use. Jackson now revved up
its engine heading for the wall, with the
last of the back-up racing onto the scene.

"He's--he's in the dozer, he's in the dozer... Kill that fucking terrorist!" Exclaimed the running driver at the top of his voice, as twenty two armoured vehicles now rolled forwards. With ground troops incoming far behind...

Two seconds later...

MUSIC MAESTRO... That was the command given by Jackson himself, as he now turned on the radio to a commercial channel. Blasting out a song playing over the Bulldozers mega phone like speakers...

Thus usually used for threats of intimidation, of racial slurs, of incoming destruction the mega phones now instead played a drum beat...

SUSSUDIO!!!!!!!!!! SUSSUDIO!!!!!!!!!! "My favorite!" Exclaimed Jackson aloud and to himself. As the Phil Collins song played onwards, blasting outwards...

A beast! A petroleum diesel drinking, gas guzzling monster. That was instantly tamed by Jackson's rippling muscular arms. As with his feet on the peddles of this vehicle. Controlled skills of mad moves and grand theft auto winning ability. Were now played out! As now dangerous and moving. He now went about putting down the Zionist

Stormtroopers truly pathetic attempts to stop to him...

Thus just like a American demolition derby. Jackson crushed and smashed the incoming vehicles. All said twenty two of them into pieces. While at the same time sparing the drivers lives... With them, themselves now escaping from the wreckage like A-Team villains... Coughing and coughing and coughing with a "Are you okay etc, etc..." While some Stormtroopers took aim, firing rapid bursts after rapid bursts!

Unmoved! Unflinching and not even blinking. Jackson did not even care as the ammunition were absorbed by the cabins bullet resistant glass. And the rest of the shots bounced of the Bulldozers bodywork! As now running rings around them all, giving them a taste of their own medicine. Making them look, no! Showing them up as the fools and misguided racist Nazi wannabe cowards that they were. Jackson knew as if he had eyes in the back his head, that a large number of more back-up troops were now on the scene in arrival. Thus leaving him to take action with Bulldozers mini guns...

EAT LEAD AND DIE, MOTHERFUCKERS... "What would be your physical reaction to getting shot?" Would it be to convulse as if you had been electrocuted? Would be to dance like a drunken spider in bodily confusion? Would it be to drop your weapon and run away like the

frighten child, like the frighten babies
that all these youths really were. As
joining up because it's the law. Not wanting
to die for Israeli, as in their heads they
finally realized that only fools die for
their country. As real patriots live for it!

Five hundred rounds later...

"Guess what? The jokes on you!!!!!!!!!!!!"
Was the look in his eyes. As being a man of
mercy! A man of principles, of rules to his
very own personal war on terror. As to him
the children of his enemy were not his
enemy. Jackson was NOT a killer of babies as
that what these young Israeli Stormtroopers
were... Just children recruited by law with
the punishment being that of prison for
refusal to serve. All collectively
brainwashed and misguided as if they were in
a cult wearing all white pajamas. Waiting
for the space ship to take them up to the
comet! With no one to tell them real right,
from real wrong... As with the dirt beneath
their feet ripped apart by the impacting
bullets, "collective compassion" was dealt
out by Jackson, who missed on purpose...

"Bring it! Be'yatch!!!!!!! Bring it!" As
with a look in his violent eyes of pure
justice that said--"You people better change
your ways RIGHT NOW! And do the TRUTH! Or
pack your SHIT UP and go hang with the Polar
Bears!" Jackson powered the Bulldozer
forward heading straight for the...

BREAKDOWN THE WALL... "No one has suffered as much as the Palestinian's have!" A quote from a man, from an "actor" running for office who then had to clarify himself with a lie! And not to tell the truth... But Jackson was no one's house boy or slave! Period! He was no liar! He was free, the only free black man. Strike that! The only FREE person in the world. Fearing no man or nation... And definitely not fearing to stand-up for truth and justice. Not in "the American way" like selectively racist fictional superheroes. But the real sense and definition of what those words mean. As now slamming and crushing apart a section of wall... Making you wonder was he actually focusing his strength through the Bulldozer itself increasing its power of destruction. As now Jackson smashed a gaping great hole into a another big hole to allow the refugees to escape!

"He did it! He did it! He broke the Wall! He can do anything!" Yelled out the little boy. While the rest of the refugees stood amazed at what they witnessed!

"Told you! He's incredible! He's incredible!" Said the young girl back with a beautiful smile. A smile that she never got to use till today!

"Let's go! Everyone--now!"

"Wait!"

THE DISTANCE RAW OF INCOMING SUPERSONIC DRONES... The said drones of robotic remotely controlled planes now zoom inwards in full formation. As therefore armed with mini guns and smart missiles galore. Setting targets to kill instantly with a sub supersonic horn blowing like echo of gunfire. Thus with Drone warfare the new tool of "civilized" peoples and said cowards. All seemed lost for the refugees. But of course it was not as the planetary patriot was in the house. So all was made instantly safe. As unleashing a quick fired volley of mini gun fire himself. Jackson acting with cool as if he was playing some old school space invaders game. Shot down all the drones without incident against the refugees themselves.

COWBOYS AND INDIANS ALL OVER AGAIN! That's what was happening. With the people of Jesus and of his virgin Mother Mary. Having the world still refusing to do right by them. With the world's false Christian and false Judaic majority getting away with murder! With genocide. With a holocaust! That's who the good people of Palestine are. That's what they have endured and still have to suffer. As running for their very lives as did every day for the past sixty plus years. (And even before that!) As being were black people in America would have been without

Martin Luther King and without the freedom riders. Along with all of the other heroes of the day. Being where Jewish people of Europe would have been if Hitler had no final solution. These brave people, these brave men, women, and these beyond brave and courageous little children. Where now on the way to safety. (For today!) As Jackson powering the Bulldozer forwards, now jumped out momentarily on top. Throwing smoke grenade canisters to increase and fully maximize the refuges escape...

"Good luck!" Whispered both the young girl and boy looking forwards. As Jackson turned gesturing victory with his two first, and second fingers pointed up high!

FIGHT THE POWER... Tell AmeriKKKa, tell not so Great Britain and any other bully. Come coward, come murdering rapist and pedophiles to FORGET themselves. Fight till you can't fight anymore--and then keep on fighting! Never give up and NEVER--never surrender! Was the silently quote that Jackson expressed, as him and the children had a moment--a silent moment of understanding. As he now turned back around, jumping into the Bulldozer. About to drive off knowing that more reinforcements would be on the way. Knowing he just had to buy them a few more minutes for them to escape...

T-Minus two minutes to launch...?

"Such a beautiful people on the outside, such a ugly people on the inside. Claiming a spiritual home on a lie, just like many other white European settlers did in the Americas and South Africa and many other places... As in possession one of man's most deadly weapons of mass destruction. That being the cheque book and pen. Israel was and is a country of pure violence and racist EVIL. With misplaced anger and vengeance against a people of colour who did nothing wrong. But call their land and rightful home Palestine..." These were just a collection of running thoughts inside Jackson's head. As he powered forwards rolling along. Only to then stop dead on a dime. Turning the Bulldozers engine off?

Incoming!!! Screamed the raw of a single HELLFIRE missile that now SLAMMED into the motionless Bulldozer! Exploding it instantaneously into a metallic flaming debris field of destruction. Making it seem so that Jackson was now officially a dead man? A very dead man!

"No way!!!" Not today or any other day to come yet!? That was the look in Jackson's almond hazel brown eyes, as he now landed down hard to the ground. Turning to seen an Apache Helicopter gunship airborne with all weapons running blazing hot. White hot!!! With what seemed like half of the Israeli Army not far behind.

"Target acquired... Guns can't lock-on?"
Yelled the Helo pilot... "Going to manual!"

Taking instant sight of the flying gunship.
Rising to his feet in directorial slow
motion. Jackson stood solid like a brick
house, like man ready to attack the said
Helicopter gunship head on...?

"Ready steady go!!!!!!!!!!!!!!!!!" Was the
call of play as Jackson now did indeed run
straight ahead. Whilst the gunship took up
an attack position heading straight for him.
Letting rip with burst after burst from its
forwards heavy machine gun...

MAN Vs MACHINE PART TWO... Bullets, bullets
and a few more hundred bullets where now
unleashed. As running straight ahead not
even dodging the incoming gunfire! And thus
showing himself to be a real life living
Superman, minus the ability to fly? Playing
the ultimate game of chicken? Jackson
continued to push forwards with the gunship
lowering its altitude to a dangerously low
level, heading forwards also...

Up! Up and NOT away he now went. As like a
champion bull fighter he now instantly
crossed paths with the speeding gunship.
That itself went by at a fast eye blinking
swiftness also. As Jackson now landed back

onto the ground... Making you think that he must have failed to stop the helicopter?

"TEMPORAL HARD RAZOR CUT!!!" He now said with cool and calm, as he stopped still and in place. Gesturing his arms in motion...

"No such thing as an unbeatable enemy." NOT EVER!!! Hezbollah proved that! And sadly will again. The counterinsurgency resistance in illegally occupied Iraq proved that! And will win! (And very disturbingly Al-Qaeda will be "allowed" to prove that as well!) And so had Jackson just proved that! Thus now walking away not even looking back, as if he knew he had been completely successful! The Helicopter gunship now continued to fly, only then to stop! Stalling in mid-flight. As if it was a toy hanging by an invisible wire. Thus with NO WAY!!! Being the call as with--"Apache down--Apache down!" Being what the pilot would of said if there was time too. But there really was no time at for any of that to be communicated. As the gunship broke apart into seven different pieces. Just like it was a block of butter that had been CUT by seven different HOT knives, at multiple angles...

Crashed down safely to Earth with its rotor blades cut down too. The smashed Gunship had slid across the ground, coming to a dead halt! As now dazed and puzzled at what just had occurred. The two pilots began to climb out. Hoping that their destructed Helicopter would not explode. Just as the final reserve of troops were coming onto their position...

"What the?" The co-pilot now said to the other. As he now witnessed Jackson running ahead and not running away, as most would expected him to do so. With the whole army in near completed approach!

T-Minus ten seconds to launch...

A CAPTURED CASTLE... Never a man to rock the boat, as he would tip it over completely. Jackson had now just leapt upwards, higher than any human being could possibly do. Landing on the wall. Doing now what he could only do in his style of defiant playful resistance. The same resistance he had delivered in nineteen seventies Northern Ireland. And nineteen eighties South Africa, and many other undeclared places throughout time too.

"ALLAHU AKBAR! ALLAHU AKBAR! ALLAHU AKBAR!!!!!!!!!!!!!!!!!!" Declared Jackson making the loudest raw any man alive could make. As thus dustin' the dirt off his shoulders. Dancing a dance of pure delight at saving so many innocent people, at saving so many innocent children! He now did "the robot" as a single gunshot rang out?

"Missed me Motherfucker... Missed me be'yatch! Ya missed!" Was the look concealed inside his ski mask. As an incoming IDF Stormtrooper had just taken a cowardly shot!

ZIONISM NO!!! JUDAISM YES!!! Was his silent quote along with "Let my people come home!" And "THAT WALL WILL FALL!" As jumping up and down in complete defiance of the arrived Stormtroopers. Jackson was now outnumbered by three hundred to one, and then some. Which was just the way he liked it! As now beyond enraged at the sight of seeing their own military compatriots beaten. Bulldozers destroyed. And their Apache Gunship down! Both men and women alike were ready to murder Jackson with extreme prejudice. Plus not to mention ready to take "trophy pictures" of his dead body afterwards with themselves in it. Just like some good old boys in the old school deep South of the U.S of A! Thus hoping to get a truly sick photo op, as too many soldiers really like to do!

Zero seconds... Launch...

With the scene of events now seeming like they were being pulled back. As if they were being filmed. All now seemed to go quiet? As a single rocket of the Katyuash style variety. ZOOMED upwards with a near and almost unheard silent swoosh... From a location not far from where Jackson had made his door opening entry!

Five seconds onwards...

Now with weapons locked and loaded, and the killing of just one human being on the cards. The Zionist Stormtroopers where about to take extreme violent action! Ready for just a normal day on the job. As without warning a single drop! Just a single drop of rain now fell, catching the lead officer in the face...

"What the?" She exclaimed wiping the rain drop of her nose, only to then catch more droplets. As the very heavens themselves thus instantly open up...

A RAIN--A REAL RAIN... "Someday a real rain will come and wash all this scum off the streets!" One of the most ultimate movie quotes of all time. And that's what was now in falling progression. As "the rain" really did fall down. As with the just used rocket containing a super piece of technology. That could make a cloudless sky rain as it had just done here! Washing away the said scum... That being not the people but the emotional poison and filth that is racism... That is Zionism! As feeling as if they were inside a power shower set to cold all of the Stormstoopers. All of the Soldiers had a strange moment of peace! Peace... That was such a strange and weird word to all involved here, as they never really thought that could ever be applied! Thus spreading like a hush on the wind itself. Peace had travelled all across the land, as Palestinian's now jumped up and down praising the almighty and the heavens. Thus enjoying the much needed rainfall.

While illegal Settlers looked through their bullet resistant windows in described ore. And everyone else from checkpoints to Tel Aviv. Stood in perfect stillness, drenched in the pitter patter of fallen clean water itself.

Ten seconds onwards...

A beautiful rain with water, water, and more water everywhere. From all directions across the whole of Gaza, Israel and the west bank of Palestine. That now fell in continuants. Thus encompassing all of the Stormtroopers and Jackson himself...

DEATH TO ISRAEL!!!? NO!!! HELL NO! PEACE TO ISRAEL! PEACE TO PALESTINE! With--"This is your home, is their home... Work something out! Peace is in your hands!" Was his standing silent message to all as Jackson now removed his ski mask. Soaked in the deluge of biblical rainfall, that was of self-descriptive monsoon portions.

Now just about to smile at his victorious completion of his mission of justice. All

was not that jovial. As having his said
smile instantly wiped of his face. Jackson's
temporal ability kicked inwards...

"So many dead! So many dead children... So
many so many dead babies..." That's what
Jackson witnessed, as standing on the wall
in complete self-silence. He was now
overcome by raw naked emotion in seeing the
"temporal echoes!" The echoes of people, of
ghosts if you will. That were themselves of
all the dead. Both innocent and guilty
individuals on both sides and in between
from the past sixty years... That now all
stood mixed up and in between. All finally
brothers and sisters. Sadly not in life but
in the death of the hereafter...

Thus now about to make his exit within a
single light splitting second. Jackson stood
taking one last look! As the rainfall
concealed his own tears... As giving them
peace for today! Peace for tomorrow was
still an unanswered question for the world
and everyone in it. That is except for
Jackson, as he was now ready to return to
tomorrow. Leaving a nation behind that has
sadly given Hitler the last laugh as he
burns in hell! With the Zionist state of
Israel standing as his greatest creation.
And as a very disturbing testament to
National Socialism. Showing that even a
large percentage of his surviving victims,
and children of his victims (And their
children after that!) are willing to embrace
his ideologies. Just as long as they find

someone else to call Nigger. Someone else to call Witch!!! Or rather someone else to call, "Jew!"

STOP THE CLOCK...

THE END

Jackson Carter will return...

www.ingramcontent.com/pod-product-compliance
Lightning Source LLC
Chambersburg PA
CBHW071213130626
46555CB00004B/1695

* 9 780956 739841 *